DESERT Dustup

BY KNIFE & PACKER

Kane Miller
A DIVISION OF EDC PUBLISHING

First American Edition 2015
Kane Miller, A Division of EDC Publishing

For information contact:
Kane Miller, A Division of EDC Publishing
P.O. Box 470663
Tulsa, OK 74147-0663
www.kanemiller.com
www.edcpub.com
www.usbornebooksandmore.com

Library of Congress Control Number: 2014950514

Manufactured by Regent Publishing Services, Hong Kong
Printed March 2015 in ShenZhen, Guangdong, China

Paperback ISBN: 978-1-61067-395-2
Hardcover ISBN: 978-1-61067-431-7

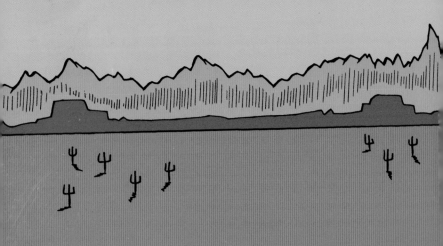

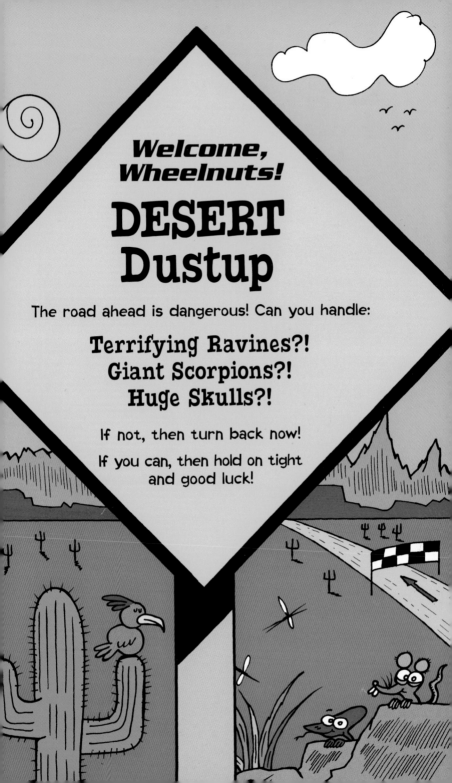

MEET THE WHEELNUTS!

Rust Bucket 3000

The Rust Bucket 3000 is the most high-tech robot car in the universe. Driven by super-sophisticated robots Nutz and Boltz, this team is always happy to use robo-gadgets to get ahead of the opposition.

The Wheel Deal

Dustin Grinner and Myley Twinkles aren't just car drivers, they are actually super-cheesy pop singers and stars of daytime TV. The Wheel Deal, their super-souped-up stretch limo, is showbiz on wheels!

Dino-Wagon

This prehistoric car is driven by the Dino-Crew——Turbo Rex and Flappy, a pterodactyl and all-around nervous passenger. Powered by an active volcano, this vehicle has a turbo boost unlike anything seen on Earth!

The Flying Diaper

Babies are great, but they are also gross, and nothing could be more gross than this pair. Gurgle and Burp are a duo of high-speed babies whose gas-powered Flying Diaper can go from zero to gross out in seconds!

The Supersonic Sparkler

Petrolnella and Dieselina (known as Nelly and Dee-Dee) are fairies with attitude, and with a sprinkling of fairy dust, the Supersonic Sparkler has a surprising turn of speed.

The Jumping Jalopy

This grandfather and grandson team drive a not-always-reliable 1930s Bugazzi. Although determined to win on skill alone, they are not above some "old-school cunning" to keep in the race.

3

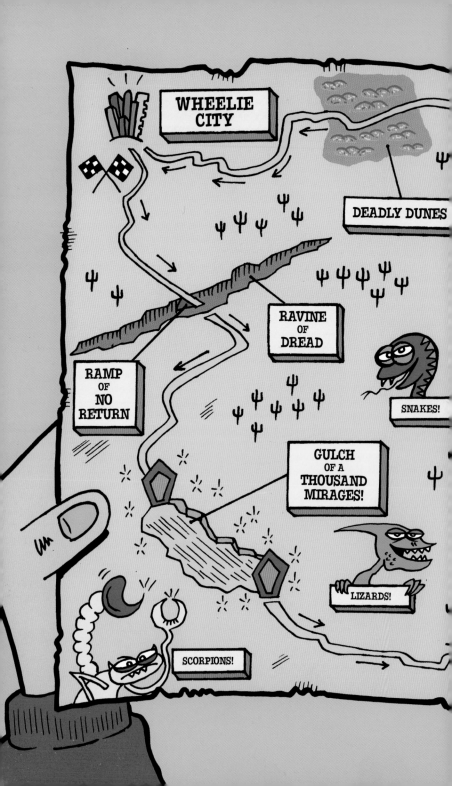

CHAPTER 1

Welcome to Wheelie City! A glitzy holiday resort built in the middle of the desert, by the man who owns most of that desert, eccentric billionaire Warren "Wheelie" Wheelnut. Wheelie City had seen some exciting things, but nothing quite as exciting as what was happening that day.

Because in the center of town was gathered the most amazing collection of cars ever. With engines growling and dust flying, the vehicles were all ready to start …

As the crowd cheered, Warren Wheelnut himself picked up the microphone to address the enormous crowd of race fans.

"Howdy, ladies and gentlemen, boys and girls—welcome to the first ever 'Wheelnuts! Craziest Race on Earth!'"

Everyone went wild. "There will be five races across some of the wildest, craziest terrains on Earth—and beyond!" he continued. "The rules are simple—there *are no* rules! Now let me introduce you to the Wheelnuts themselves!"

As the cars revved up their engines, Wheelie introduced each team and asked what they thought of the desert course.

"First up we have the Dino-Wagon!"

We're going to ROAR into the lead! GRRRRR!!!

We're so confident we've brought our pails and shovels!

"Next, the Wheel Deal!"

If we see any nasty rattlesnakes we'll charm them with our singing ...

Buuuuuuuuuuuuuurp!

"Over here we have the Flying Diaper!"

We plan to dazzle in the desert!

"Next up, the Supersonic Sparkler!"

Go, Team Fairy!

"And last, but by no means least, we have the Rust Bucket 3000!"

I compute that this terrain is very similar to the Benyon Plains of planet Octagon 7!

So there we have it, ladies and gentlemen. Now please give a *Wheelie* big round of applause for the Wheelnuts!

"Now I know that all of you want to win and we have big shiny trophies for the top three drivers," said Wheelie. "But to make the race even more exciting there are Wheelnut Gold Stars to be won at checkpoints and in the world-famous Wheelnut Challenge. And those stars aren't just to make you feel pleased with yourselves, oh no! You can use these stars at the Wheelnut Garage to improve your car. You can buy new gadgets, cheats or even just make your car a little more comfortable. So make sure you whip up a sandstorm on the desert track I have prepared for you!"

Wheelie was about to start the race when one of his assistants handed him a note.

"A late entry? I thought *these* were the only cars crazy enough to take on my race. Bring 'em on!" said the excited billionaire.

There was a loud bang and an ancient race car emerged from a cloud of smoke.

"Race fans, I give you," spluttered Wheelie, glancing at the note, "the Jumping Jalopy—Campbell and his grandson James in their vintage Bugazzi …"

"Sorry we're late, Mr. Wheelnut," mumbled James.

"There's no time for excuses, partners," interrupted Wheelie. "We've got racing to do!"

Wheelie pulled the cord on the enormous starter cannon, there was a ground-shuddering BANG! and the contestants were off! The Craziest Race on Earth was underway and it was soon going to get a whole lot crazier!

The crowd went wild as the cars screeched to the first turn. It seemed they were all taking turns to hold first place—first the Dino-Wagon, then the Supersonic Sparkler before the Flying Diaper burst into the lead.

But as the cars sped off, it became clear that one car had not even started the race.

CHAPTER 2

The Rust Bucket 3000!

"We appear to have a transmodulator interruption in the cronium bicobulator," said Nutz in a robotic voice. "It has caused axelated damage to the rear corresponder valve …"

"So what you're saying is?" said Boltz.

"We've got a screw loose … and damaged a vital engine piece," said Nutz. "We'll need to get one sent from our home planet. According to the garage on Zantium 6 it could take a year …"

"A year!" gasped Boltz. "The race will be over by then!"

"A Zantium year, you metallic fool," said Nutz. "That's about twenty minutes on Earth. The garage will track us down and deliver the part wherever we are on the course."

"So we're still in the race! Groovy!" cried Boltz, high-fiving his metal buddy.

"Yes, but we're not going anywhere right now," said Nutz. "We need to do *something* to keep up with the other racers."

"What about catching a bus?" asked Boltz.

"Leave the ideas to me, you ridiculous rivet," said Nutz. "We need to patch up the Rust Bucket ..."

"OK, so the rear corresponder valve is basically a long, thin metal rod," said Boltz, trying to be helpful. "And where could we find one of those?"

While Nutz and Boltz look for a spare part to get going, let's take a closer look at their car as we put the Rust Bucket 3000 UNDER THE SPOTLIGHT!

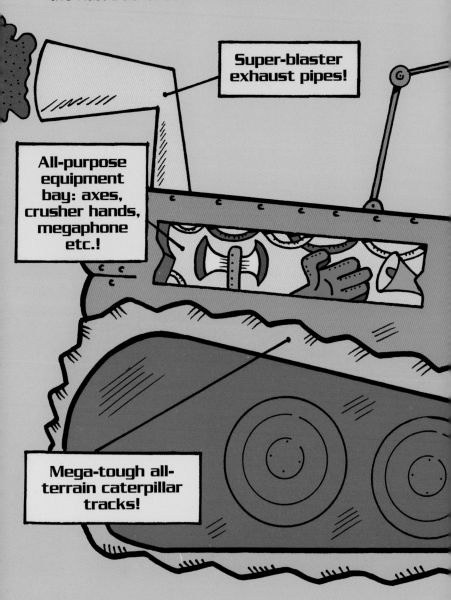

Super-blaster exhaust pipes!

All-purpose equipment bay: axes, crusher hands, megaphone etc.!

Mega-tough all-terrain caterpillar tracks!

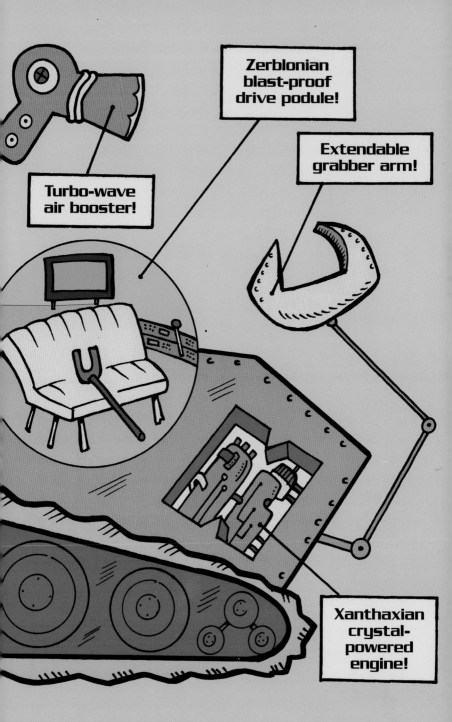

Turbo-wave air booster!

Zerblonian blast-proof drive podule!

Extendable grabber arm!

Xanthaxian crystal-powered engine!

Nutz turned to the onboard computer to analyze the objects around them. They were about to give up when all of a sudden the machine started beeping and flashing.

"What have you got?" asked Boltz excitedly.

"The perfect fit!" said Nutz. "That old lady's cane! I hope she'll lend it to us …"

"This is simply so exciting!" said the old lady as the Rust Bucket tried to catch up with the other cars. Mrs. Paterson, as it turned out was her name, had been happy to lend them her cane on the condition it was never out of her sight!

"I just hope that cane holds up, Mrs. Paterson," said Nutz.

"At least we're moving," said Boltz. "Even if we are in last place …"

Ahead of them the racers were still burning rubber on the winding streets of Wheelie City. No car could hold on to a lead and whenever one got ahead the others were able to catch up.

The Rust Bucket was starting to make good progress and they could now see the dust and hear the engines of the cars up ahead.

"We're catching up!" said an excited Boltz.

"But we're still in last place," said Nutz.

But the Rust Bucket 3000 wasn't going to be in last place for long because ahead of them one of the cars was about to pull over.

"Hey; Myley, this is soooo coool," said Dustin Grinner, the singing sensation from the boy band One Way Traffic. "Are you thinking what I'm thinking?"

"You'd better believe it," said Myley Twinkles. "All of these boutiques—let's shop!"

"I could soooo use a new outfit!" chuckled the cheesy singer.

As the Wheel Deal pulled over the rest of the cars were in no mood for shopping.

"Let's see what these other racers have got!" said Turbo Rex in the Dino-Wagon.

Flappy pushed up a dial on the dashboard and the volcano that powered the vehicle began to splutter noisily.

"Hold tight!" cried Flappy as the car took off onto the desert track outside the city.

"See you later, losers!"

CHAPTER 3

So as the drivers zoomed out of the bustling town and powered into the desert, the Dino-Wagon was barely in front. But out in the desert the only spectators were a bit of wildlife and the occasional cactus ... and a cactus doesn't really see much—or does it?

Let's take a closer look at that cactus over there, the big one by the road ...

"Look at them go!" said a man in a cactus suit. "Aren't they all so clever in their fancy cars!"

In case you're wondering, the man in the cactus suit is Waylon "Wipeout" Wheelnut. He's actually Warren's twin brother ...

From a young age Warren and Waylon competed against each other ... and Warren was always just that little bit faster ...

When they grew up they both built vacation resorts ... but unlike glitzy and successful Wheelie City, Waylon's Wipeoutville is deserted, infested with rats and falling to pieces ...

Wipeout also runs a race—it's called "Wipeout's Silliest Race on Earth," but no one enters it ...

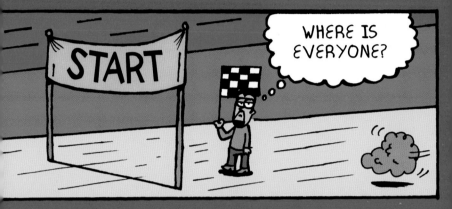

But Wipeout is convinced both his race and his resort can be a success if he can just get rid of the competition. Starting by wrecking Wheelie's race ...

Dipstick, Wipeout's evil sidekick, now piped up as a final car appeared over the horizon. "Hey, look, Mr. Wipeout, sir, there's a straggler—quick, hide!" Dipstick was dressed as a fence post.

"It's those singing nincompoops Twinkles and Grinner," whispered Wipeout. "For goodness' sake, don't move!"

But Myley and Dustin had spotted them and didn't find the situation at all strange.

"Why hello there, talking cactus and talking fence post," said Myley. "Wheelie did warn us this route was crazy! We need to catch up with the other racers, can you show us which way they went?"

"We'll sing for you if you tell us," added Dustin. "Look, we've got new spangly outfits and everything." He cleared his throat …

"No, no, no! Please don't sing! They went that way!" Wipeout barked, and breathed a sigh of relief as the Wheel Deal headed off again.

"Now we have to stop this race," said Wipeout. "We need it to be a total disaster … have you done what I told you?"

"Yes, sir," said Dipstick. "We had our top scientists working on the project. The *creatures* should be delivered any minute!"

Wipeout and Dipstick then both let out an evil laugh …

Hahaha hahaha hahaha hahaha ha…

CHAPTER 4

Meanwhile, with the Wheel Deal now back in the main group, all the cars were wrestling for position.

"That's the trouble with desert courses," said Campbell. "Too flat. Not much of a challenge!"

"I'm not so sure about that, Grandpa," said James, pointing ahead. "Look!"

The teams gasped as they saw what faced them—a huge ravine with only one narrow ramp over it!

RAMP OF
NO RETURN

The race was really on now, as the cars jostled for position in an attempt to be first across the ramp …

The Supersonic Sparkler swerved to the front, sprinkling pink fairy dust behind them … but this wasn't any old fairy dust.

"It's Instant Itchy Dust!" cackled Nelly.

"And it gets EVERYWHERE!" chuckled Dee-Dee.

Cars swerved as the drivers struggled to cope with the itchy dust.

"It's in my moustache!" said Campbell as he tried to scratch and drive at the same time.

"Hey, it's all over our new outfits!" moaned Myley.

"I didn't think robots could get itchy!" said Nutz.

"This itching is fun-nnnneee!" chortled Gurgle in the Flying Diaper.

But one car wasn't affected by the itching powder. With their superthick leathery skin the Dino-Wagon crew was finding the whole thing hilarious. But they stopped laughing when they saw that the Supersonic Sparkler was going to be the first to cross the ravine …

"We can't let this happen!" said Turbo Rex. "Time for some Volcano Power!"

Now the thing about the volcano at the back of the Dino-Wagon was that not only did it provide the engine with its power … but it was also home to all kinds of prehistoric creatures!

CHAPTER 5

"**I** know what to do!" said Flappy. "These pterodactyls will FLY us across!" Just then, a flock of pterodactyls flapped out of the volcano.

"Now wing us over that ravine!" said Turbo Rex. But the pterodactyls had other ideas—instead of lifting the Dino-Wagon into the air they started pecking at the other racers! Soon there were pterodactyls flapping all over the course, and some cars were better equipped to deal with them than others …

"I should warn you that we have serious burp power!" said Gurgle in the Flying Diaper.

"Take that, you nasty, nasty birds!" shouted Burp as the Flying Diaper let off ground-shuddering burps. The pterodactyls had had enough and flapped away coughing and spluttering.

Next under attack was the Rust Bucket 3000. "What creatures are these?" asked Nutz. "My computer does not recognize them."

"Are there no dinosaurs on your home planet?" asked the old lady. "Funnily enough there aren't supposed to be any on ours. They vanished millions of years ago."

"Well how do we get rid of these 'dinosaurs'?" asked Boltz.

"Let me have my cane," said Mrs. Paterson.

The Rust Bucket 3000 pulled over and Mrs. Paterson was soon scaring off the pterodactyls with her cane.

"Hey! Careful with that rear corresponder valve!" said Nutz. "We still need it."

"Get away, you oversized pigeons!" cried the old lady, whirling her cane above her head.

With all the pterodactyls scared away from their car the robots could get back in the race.

At the front of the race it was now between the Dino-Wagon and the Supersonic Sparkler for who would be first across the ravine—and the two were frantically jostling for position.

"Get away, you leathery fiends!" cried Nelly.

"You are soooo un-sparkly!" wailed Dee-Dee. "Nelly, hit the Fly Button!"

As you've probably noticed, the Supersonic Sparkler is shaped like a butterfly and is capable of short bursts of flight.

"You'll never catch us!" cackled Dee-Dee as they started to flutter across the ravine.

But the Dino-Crew was not going to give up that easily, and their pterodactyls were helping them to catch up with the fairy duo.

"We're crossing that ravine first!" cried Turbo Rex. "It's time to play dirty!"

"You don't mean???" Flappy gulped.

"You'd better believe it!" said Turbo Rex.

Now, as we mentioned before, in the Craziest Race on Earth there are no rules, and what was about to happen is not something we will make excuses for. So if you're easily offended, look away now—because on the next page is a "SUPER-SICK MEGA-NAUGHTY CHEAT."

SUPER-SICK MEGA-NAUGHTY CHEAT!

Turbo Rex gave the order and two of the pterodactyls swooped off in the direction of the Supersonic Sparkler ... and started biting it!

"Hey, what are these disgusting creatures doing to our lovely sparkly vehicle?" screeched Dee-Dee.

"I'm losing control!" cried Nelly.

As the Supersonic Sparkler tried to evade the pterodactyls the Dino-Wagon crossed the ravine in first place!

The Supersonic Sparkler crossed next and then the other cars all shot across on the ramp. The Wheelnuts had reached the first race checkpoint. And there to meet them was Warren "Wheelie" Wheelnut himself!

"Howdy and congratulations, drivers! That was some mighty fine driving … and some really mean cheatin'! Let's see who earned the most Gold Stars!"

Ravine Checkpoint

1	Dino-Wagon 6 stars
2	Supersonic Sparkler 5 stars
3	Jumping Jalopy 4 stars
4	Flying Diaper 3 stars
5	Wheel Deal 2 stars
6	Rust Bucket 3000 1 star

The stars: 6 stars for first place, 5 stars for second place, 4 stars for third place, 3 stars for fourth place, 2 stars for fifth place and 1 star for sixth place.

CHAPTER 6

Although the drivers were pleased to take a break this wasn't going to be a long rest.

"Now if you can all step out of your vehicles I will explain the first ever 'Wheelnut Challenge,'" said Wheelie as he led the drivers to a specially constructed, glittery archway. "This challenge couldn't be simpler. All you need to do is follow the path to the other side."

"I thought this was meant to be a *challenge*," scoffed Dustin. "We can walk *and* perform some of our platinum-selling hits as we go …"

"I haven't told you the name of the challenge yet," said Wheelie ominously. "You are about to enter the Gulch of a Thousand Mirages."

The drivers all went quiet—this sounded a bit scarier than a walk in the desert.

"Excuse me, but what's a 'mirage'?" asked Gurgle.

"It's when you think you see something that isn't actually there," said Wheelie. "You'll know when you see one … this challenge is all about who can last longest. When you've had enough just shout, 'I'm a Wheelnut, get me out of here!'"

The drivers nervously entered the Gulch of a Thousand Mirages and at once everything was not as it seemed … but instead of scary things, it was food that started to appear! Everyone's favorites were there—the Dino-Wagon crew was soon drooling at a huge triceratops steak, and James and Campbell were being distracted by burgers and fries …

I got to get me some meat—I'm a Wheelnut, get me out of here!

Nelly and Dee-Dee were face-to-face with a huge pink cupcake. This was too much for them!

With two sets of drivers knocked out, the rest of the Wheelnuts carried on farther into the gulch. They hadn't expected food—so what could possibly be next? Well if the drivers' efforts had made them hungry, the desert heat had certainly made them thirsty! *Really* thirsty!

Soon great fountains of icy cold water were springing up everywhere. Raging rivers of water swirled all around them! But the trouble was … none of the water was real! Soon the drivers were starting to crack.

The only drivers who were still in the Gulch of a Thousand Mirages were the crew of the Rust Bucket 3000—robots don't drink water, only oil— and the Flying Diaper. Like most babies, they only drink milk. But the next mirage was the hardest to handle yet … with the drivers feeling tired what could be more tempting than a bed! Who would fall asleep first?

No matter how hard they tried the Flying Diaper team just couldn't keep going …

I'm a … yawn … Wheelnut, get me out of here …

Fortunately robots don't need sleep …

That left the Rust Bucket robots as the winners!

The challenge was over and the drivers reassembled by their cars. After all the temptations of the Gulch of a Thousand Mirages everyone had a chance for something real to eat and drink … but there was no time for sleep!

CHAPTER 7

Soon enough the drivers were back doing what they did best: racing! And once again the course started off nice and easy … but this time the drivers were all suspicious about what was going to come next. All except one!

"I like it," said Campbell as they sped into an early lead. "Clear open roads, not a ravine in sight."

"Please don't say that, Grandpa," begged James. It seemed that every time Campbell got relaxed something dangerous happened …

Sure enough, as they drove on it became much harder to see. A dust storm was swirling and they were right in the middle of it!

"Get the spotlight on!" shouted Myley, who was driving the Wheel Deal. Dustin pointed the spotlight at the road, but even under the powerful beam it was invisible.

"Hey, is it me or are we slowing down?" asked Dee-Dee.

"Forget slowing down—I think we're sinking!" wailed Nelly.

In the middle of the dust storm the cars hadn't seen the warning signs, and were all sinking into quicksand!

The cars were starting to sink, and no matter how hard the drivers tried, no one could move. Then Burp in the Flying Diaper had an idea …"If we can't *drive* through this quicksand then maybe we can *float* through!"

"Are you thinking what I'm thinking?" replied Gurgle.

"RIVER OF DROOL!!!" they cried.

The other drivers closed their windows and tried to stay dry as the babies gurgled up a river of drool!

In no time the Wheelnuts were sweeping through the quicksand zone and onward, with the Flying Diaper way out in front.

"Thanks, Gurgle and Burp," said Turbo Rex as the Dino-Wagon tried to nudge them off the road.

"You're welcome!" said Gurgle as their car burped a toxic cloud at the prehistoric pair.

CHAPTER 8

But up ahead something even more dangerous was about to happen. A helicopter carrying a huge cargo container was hovering into view. Wipeout was back on the scene!

"Your team of scientists did a great job, sir," said Dipstick.

"They better had—I paid them enough!" barked Wipeout. "Now all we need to do is find the perfect ambush spot for my little beauties …"

The helicopter scanned the horizon. "Over there! The road is narrow as it goes between those two mountains," he said gleefully. "Now land the chopper!"

Dipstick soon landed the helicopter in the chosen spot.

Next the two villains untied the large cargo box
—everything was in position.

"All we have to do is wait for the drivers to come
along, we open this box and the race is over!"
chuckled Wipeout.

"Then the world will have to watch *your* race,"
said Dipstick.

"And my brother will be ruined!" cackled
Wipeout.

CHAPTER 9

As the cars approached, all they were thinking about was their position in the race.

"C'mon, Grandpa, you can do it!" said James as they tried to get past the Supersonic Sparkler.

Up front the Dino-Wagon and the Flying Diaper were still locked wheel-to-wheel as they flew around the corner, and what they saw next chilled them to the tips of their exhaust pipes …

Huge robotic scorpions were blocking the road!

"I know we were told this was a dangerous track, but no one mentioned giant metal beasties!" said Nelly.

High above in the hills a man with a remote control was cackling.

"This is too easy!" chuckled Wipeout. "Each scorpion's sting has enough rust venom to disable sixty cars. Wheelie, your race is about to be over FOREVER!!!"

James noticed a small opening in the cliffs … it had to be worth a try.

"Quick—in here!" he shouted as the Wheelnuts quickly shot through the gap. Last in was the Dino-Wagon, and Turbo Rex managed to nudge a few boulders in front of the entrance.

"This should block the scorpions for a little bit," said Turbo Rex. "But we need to think of something fast!"

The Wheelnuts were now all backed up against a sheer cliff face, and the scorpions were slowly starting to smash through the rocks!

All of a sudden there was a flash of light and a huge spaceship appeared overhead!

"It's a miracle!" cried Campbell.

"Aliens from another planet have arrived to save us!" screeched Nelly.

"Let's sing them a welcoming song," said Myley before beginning to warble. "*Aliens, from another planet …*"

"Actually, guys," said Nutz, "they're robot mechanics, from Zantium 6."

"It's our rear corresponder valve!" said Boltz.

The spaceship gently landed and at once the mechanics got to work on the Rust Bucket 3000.

"Mission accomplished," said the robot mechanic. "We must depart …"

"Could you do one more job for us?" said Nutz. "Take Mrs. Paterson home?"

Mrs. Paterson, who didn't think her day could get any more exciting, was now getting a lift home in a spaceship!

But as the drivers waved her farewell Flappy piped up. "It's time for some Wheelnuts teamwork!"

Now you will have noticed the Wheelnuts were incredibly competitive with each other. And they would stop at nearly nothing to win a race, but if there was one thing they wouldn't tolerate it was a threat to the Craziest Race on Earth. There was no way they were going to allow Wipeout and his mechanical menaces to stop the competition.

"We need a plan and we need one fast!" said Campbell.

"Gather around!" said a robotic voice. It was Boltz.

"We are robots too," said Nutz, "and we have an idea as to how we can stop these creatures—it's going to be tough, but we don't have time for anything else."

Sure enough, the robot scorpions were scratching their way through the boulders!

CHAPTER 10

The Wheelnuts were all now in position.
"The trap is set," whispered Nutz.
"Let's hope it works!" whispered Boltz.
Just then the giant scorpions managed to dislodge the final boulder and burst through. But instead of finding the Wheelnuts trembling in fear, they found … nothing!

"NOW!" shouted Nutz.

It was time for the Wheelnuts' ambush and everyone knew exactly what they had to do.

First of all, James had to leap in front of the scorpions to lure them to the back of the cave ...

Here the Dino-Wagon blocked their path ...

As they tried to use their stingers, the Supersonic Sparkler team sprinkled them with Tickle Dust ...

When the scorpions tried to back away, Gurgle and Burp dribbled on their wheels, making them rust ...

Finally, when they couldn't move, Nutz and Boltz located their oil containers and drained them ...

There was a loud fizzing noise—without oil the scorpions were simply lumps of useless metal!

"Great job, everyone!" cried Nutz. "Those heaps of metal won't be troubling anyone ever again!"

High in the hills above, Wipeout could not believe what he had just seen.

"Confound the Wheelnuts and confound my brother!" screeched the nasty man.

"We'd better get out of here," said Dipstick as they ran for the helicopter.

"I'll get you next time!" screeched Wipeout as he swooped away over the desert.

"Well, that was close," said Nutz.

"Now let's get back to racing!" said Campbell.

The cars all revved up and were back on the course—after the forced break all the drivers were more desperate than ever to hit the road!

CHAPTER 11

The road swept down from the hills and into a gorge—the sides of the mountains seemed to be closing in as the cars jostled for position.

Cruising along quietly at the back of the pack were Myley and Dustin—but they were about to get a lot louder. The showbiz dream team decided it was time to make their BIG move.

"OK, Dustin," said Myley, who was at the wheel of the car. "Over to you!"

Dustin climbed out through the sunroof and onto the roof of the car.

"Make sure your safety harness is secure!" shouted Myley. "Now give it everything you've got!"

Even for a showbiz veteran like Dustin, singing on top of a speeding car on a desert track was tricky. But this was their big moment in the race and Dustin started to belt out the number one hit, *Bumper Sticker of Love!*

The other cars all jolted at this sudden bolt of high-decibel cheesy noise, but what was about to follow was far worse than the sound of Dustin's singing. His high-pitched warbling had fractured some massive boulders and they were starting to rumble downhill and across the road!

"It's working, Myley!" shouted Dustin. "Now crank up your microphone and join me in the chorus."

Myley didn't even have to let go of the steering wheel as she pressed the "on" button on her mic.

You driiiiiiiiiive me
wiiiiiiiiiild!!!!

Colossal chunks of rock crashed onto the course, the other vehicles swerving madly to get out of the way! It was easy for the Wheel Deal to avoid the bunch and speed away. It now had a clear road ahead and not another car in sight!

"That's how *we* roll!" bellowed Dustin.

"Leaving that talentless crowd waaaay out of sight!" Myley added.

If they hadn't been gloating so much they might have noticed the road sign at the entrance to a tunnel up ahead …

"Hey, it's dark in here," said Myley as their car entered the tunnel. "Turn the spotlight to the forward position." Dustin swung the spotlight around and they drove on and on for what felt like forever.

Finally, in the distance, they could just about make out a small dot of light.

"Nearly there," said Dustin. "It's kind of creepy in here—I think it's time for a song!"

CHAPTER 12

Myley flattened the accelerator and they burst out of the tunnel and into a really weird world. Suddenly Dustin didn't feel like singing!

"This place is sc-sc-scary!" wailed Myley.

"There are skulls everywhere!" said a shaking Dustin.

But there was no going back. In fact, Myley heard a noise that got the Wheel Deal back on course.

"I can hear the other cars," said Myley. "They must have gotten around the boulders."

"Hit it!" said Dustin.

Tunnel Checkpoint

1	Wheel Deal	6 stars
2	Rust Bucket 3000	5 stars
3	Dino-Wagon	4 stars
4	Jumping Jalopy	3 stars
5	Flying Diaper	2 stars
6	Supersonic Sparkler	1 star

The stars: 6 stars for first place, 5 stars for second place, 4 stars for third place, 3 stars for fourth place, 2 stars for fifth place and 1 star for sixth place.

The Wheel Deal zoomed forward again, but, as Myley feared, it wasn't long before the other Wheelnuts were in hot pursuit.

"I assume the skulls are purely for decoration," said Nelly to Dee-Dee as they tried to keep up with the Rust Bucket 3000.

But this was a Warren "Wheelie" Wheelnut race course and nothing was there "purely for decoration." The skulls seemed to be alive and were chasing after the vehicles. Myley and Dustin were first in line for some *skull*duggery—one huge skull was snapping at the rear of the Wheel Deal!

"This is just so *not* red carpet!" complained Dustin as he desperately tried to fight off the skull. "It's going to nibble my shiny showbiz shoes."

In a desperate bid to steer clear of the skull, Myley had driven the limo off the road!

But there was more to come.

Soon skulls started rolling across the road!

"Hold tight!" shouted Campbell. "I've seen all kinds of things during my racing career, but skulls on a road?! This is a first!"

"Burp them out of the way!" bawled Gurgle. But there were just too many and the Jumping Jalopy and Flying Diaper were swerving all over the place as they tried to stay in the race.

However, things were even worse for the Dino-Wagon and the Supersonic Sparkler—they had been swallowed up whole by a gigantic skull!

"We're trapped!" bellowed Turbo Rex.

"Don't tell me this skull is sparkle-proof!" squealed Nelly.

The only car that was getting away was the Rust Bucket 3000.

"With our new rear corresponder valve in place we're unstoppable!" chortled Nutz.

"No stupid skull can stop US from winning!" scoffed Boltz.

But the robotic racers had spoken too soon …

"Is it me or are we floating?" said Nutz as they began to rise up into the air. Boltz looked down to see that they were being carried on the top of a giant hot air skull!

CHAPTER 13

With the Wheelnuts floating, swerving and skidding all over the place, one spectator in particular was having a great time—Warren "Wheelie" Wheelnut himself!

"This is darn tootin' marvelous!" said Wheelie as he operated the controls in front of him. "I just knew Skull Valley would sort out the real racers from the weekend drivers! Yeeeee-haaaw!!!"

Wheelie had been controlling the skulls all along! "Now let's see who'll be first to escape my animatronic skulls!" he chuckled.

To get away from the snapping skull, Dustin had to give up his shiny new shoes!

So long, shoes!

The Jumping Jalopy and Flying Diaper found the only way to get around the rolling skulls was to use the Bugazzi snowplow and drive through them.

Inside the giant skull, the Supersonic Sparkler and Dino-Wagon tried to use the volcano to blast them out, but when that failed the butterfly wings finally managed to tickle the jaws open.

And finally on the floating skull, high in the sky, the Rust Bucket 3000 had to throw out an anchor to bring them back to Earth.

Good thing we have the hardware to handle zero gravity driving!

The Wheelnuts were finally free from Skull Valley and the race was back on. One by one they burst onto the main track and back towards Wheelie City.
And with the checkered flag practically in touching distance, the gloves really were about to come off!

CHAPTER 14

The final part of the race was across a series of huge sand dunes … well, we say "sand," but this is the Craziest Race on Earth and sand would be far too boring. Warren "Wheelie" Wheelnut had one final trick up his sleeve. The first car to notice that something was up was the Supersonic Sparkler …

"Hey, these pink dunes are *so* pretty!" said Nelly. "You could say they're delicious."

"But why are we slowing down?" said Dee-Dee. "In fact, why is *everyone* slowing down? And is it just me or is it getting cold in here?"

As the Bugazzi struggled to move, James couldn't help but scoop up a handful of the pink "sand," and when he had a closer look it turned out to be exactly what he'd guessed.

"Strawberry ice cream!" said James, spooning it up.

"Deee-licious!" said Campbell. "But it's not going to help us to win the race."

Indeed none of the vehicles were built for this kind of edible terrain. The race had ground to a halt!

It was the Dino-Wagon that finally got back on track.

"Fire up the volcano to superhot!" said Turbo Rex.

"OK, it's now hot enough to toast a stegosaurus sandwich!" said Flappy.

As Turbo Rex had hoped, the ice cream started to melt and they were able to zoom through.

The prehistoric pair were out in front, but the other Wheelnuts quickly used the path cleared by the Dino-Wagon to get back on course.

The cars were now speeding towards Wheelie City and it was everyone for themselves …

The Wheel Deal tried to distract the Rust Bucket 3000 with an impromptu dance number.

The Flying Diaper tried to upend the Supersonic Sparkler with a burp, while the Dino-Wagon attempted to nose the Jumping Jalopy off the course with a blast of volcano dust.

And as the checkered flag loomed into view the Dino-Wagon dashed to the front …

CHAPTER 15

And won by a whisker as the crowd went wild!!! The other drivers pulled up, exhausted but delighted to have completed the course. And there to meet them was Warren "Wheelie" Wheelnut!

Congratulations, Wheelnuts, on making the Desert Dustup race such a great competition! There was sneakiness, cheating and some downright naughty driving—I LOVED IT!!!

As the applause from the crowd died down the first three cars took their places on the podium.

"It's time for the trophy presentation," said Wheelie. "In third place, we have the Wheel Deal—you get the Rattlesnake Medal."

"In second place is the Rust Bucket 3000— you get the Coyote Cup … and in first place, receiving the Desert Dustup Trophy … it's the Dino-Wagon!!!"

But as Wheelie reached to get the trophy, disaster …

"I think I left it at home!" confessed the embarrassed billionaire.

Fortunately one of the cars was making an urgent call …

There was a flash of light and once again a large spaceship loomed into view.

"We picked up the trophy and have it right here!" said a robot mechanic.

"Luckily we travel at three times the speed of light!"

Warren "Wheelie" Wheelnut was finally able to hand over the Desert Dustup Trophy and the crowd went wild …

"Well, that's all for this race," said Wheelie as the applause died down. "And don't forget you all have lots of Gold Stars to spend in the Wheelnut Garage."

"I think we should buy an onboard freezer," said Flappy. "It would be great to have some ice cream we can actually eat!"

"Ice cream on the move? Tasty!" chuckled Wheelie. "But don't forget the second race starts soon! Join us for Race 2 in the Craziest Race on Earth!"

Turn over for a sneak peek of the next course …

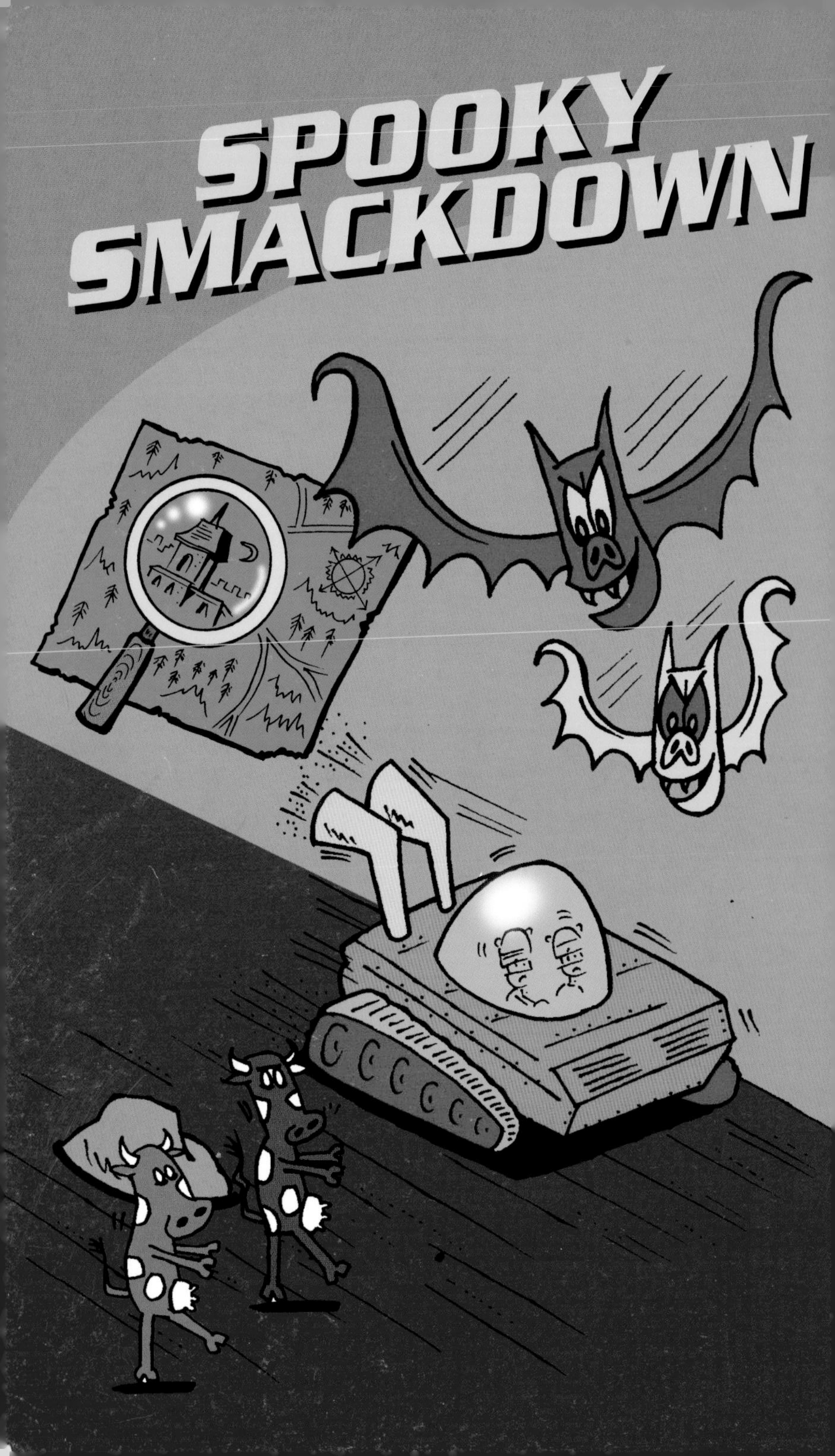
SPOOKY
SMACKDOWN